SPORTING CHAMPIONSHIPS
Boston Marathon

Blaine Wiseman

WEIGL PUBLISHERS INC.
"Creating Inspired Learning"
www.weigl.com

Published by Weigl Publishers Inc.
350 5th Avenue, 59th Floor
New York, NY 10118

Website: www.weigl.com

Library of Congress Cataloging-in-Publication Data available upon request.
Fax 1-866-44-WEIGL for the attention of the Publishing Records department.

ISBN 978-1-61690-124-0 (hard cover)
ISBN 978-1-61690-125-7 (soft cover)

Printed in the United States of America in North Mankato, Minnesota
1 2 3 4 5 6 7 8 9 0 14 13 12 11 10

052010
WEP264000

Weigl acknowledges Getty Images as its primary image supplier for this title.

Project Coordinator
Heather C. Hudak

Design
Terry Paulhus

CONTENTS

What is the Boston Marathon?

The Boston Marathon is the oldest, most-recognized **annual** marathon in the world. Each year, thousands of people from all over the world gather to run 26 miles, 385 yards (42.2 kilometers) from Hopkinton, Massachusetts, to the Back Bay section of Boston. Running a marathon is a great achievement, and the Boston Marathon is the biggest marathon of them all.

Thought to be one of the world's greatest fitness and endurance challenges, the Boston Marathon is organized by the Boston Athletic Association (B.A.A.). The association has hosted the marathon and other athletic events in Boston for more than 100 years. The goal of the B.A.A. is to encourage people to live a healthy lifestyle by participating in sports. Running is the sport of choice for the B.A.A.

People train for months, or even years, to compete in the Boston Marathon.

CHANGES THROUGHOUT THE YEARS

Past	Present
In 1897, 15 runners competed, and 10 finished.	In 2009, 26,167 people competed, with 22,843 finishing.
In 1947, the world marathon record was set in Boston at 2:25:39 (2 hours, 25 minutes, and 39 seconds).	The winner of the 2010 Boston Marathon finished in 2:05:52.
The first time that a woman finished the race was in 1966.	In 2009, 9,298 women crossed the finish line.
In 1975, a wheelchair division was included in the Boston Marathon. Bob Hall finished in 2:58:00.	In 2009, 34 people participated in the Boston Marathon wheelchair division.
In 1975, Liane Winter finished the marathon in 2:42:24, a world record for women.	In 2002, Margaret Okayo set a record when she finished the Boston Marathon in 2:20:43.

The Champions' Trophy

The Boston Marathon Champions' Trophy was first presented in 2000. The 47.5-inch (121-centimeter) **sterling** silver cup is attached to a base of **mahogany**. It displays the names of each champion since the very first Boston Marathon. It also has room to add the names of every champion for 100 more years.

Boston Marathon History

In 490 BC, a soldier named Pheidippides ran from a battlefield in the town of Marathon, Greece, to the nation's capital, Athens. When he arrived, Pheidippides said to the leaders, "Rejoice! We conquer!," before he collapsed and died of **exhaustion**. Marathons get their name from this story. In 1896, the first **modern** Olympics took place in Athens. The first marathon race was held at this event.

In March 1887, a group of sports enthusiasts, **entrepreneurs**, and politicians formed the B.A.A. The purpose of the association was to promote physical activity in Boston. The group hosted sporting events, such as boxing, fencing, and track and field.

The original B.A.A. clubhouse contained a gymnasium, a billiard hall, a bowling alley, and tennis courts. The club began hosting road races in 1890, and seven years later, it hosted its first marathon. John Graham, the manager of the American Olympic team in 1896, was a member of the B.A.A. He was so inspired by the Olympic marathon that he decided to hold one the following year in Boston. It was called the B.A.A. Road Race. Later, it would become known as the Boston Marathon.

Athens hosted the Olympics in 1896 and 2004. The 2004 Olympic marathon began in Marathon.

People first began training for marathons in the late 1800s.

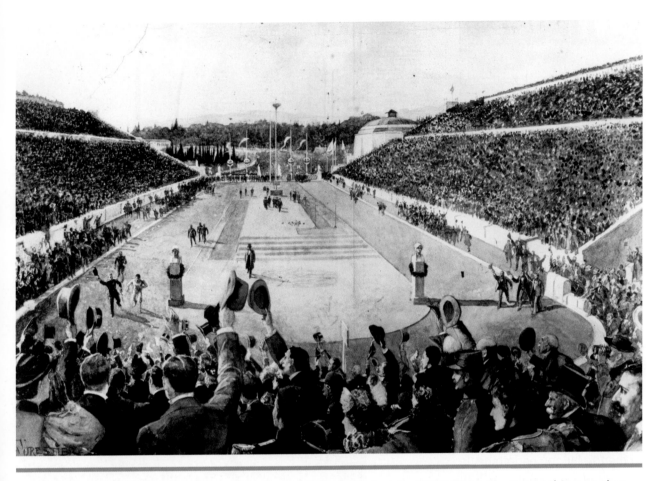

Spyridon Louis won the first modern marathon in Athens during the 1896 Olympics. It was this race that inspired John Graham to hold a marathon in his home city of Boston.

The First Marathon Race

The first marathon race retraced the steps of Pheidippides, from Marathon Bridge to the Olympic Stadium in Athens. The marathon's distance was set at 24.85 miles (40 km). This was the accepted distance for a marathon until 1908, when London, England, hosted the Olympics. The race started at Windsor Castle and finished in front of the king at the Olympic Stadium. This changed the official distance of a marathon to 26 miles, 385 yards (41.195 km).

Rules of the Run

The rules of a marathon are simple. The goal is for a marathon runner to finish the race as fast as possible. Marathons challenge people to push their body to extremes. Many people know they will not place in the top spots. They are happy to reach the finish line. Others challenge themselves to finish within a certain time frame. For **elite** runners, the goal of running is to win the marathon.

1 Divisions

There are several divisions in the Boston Marathon, with a winner from each division. The divisions include women's open, men's open, men's masters, women's masters, men's wheelchair, and women's wheelchair. The winner of each division gets his or her name engraved on the Champions' Trophy. In addition to the trophy, top performers in the marathon, including **mobility impaired** and **visually impaired** division winners, win awards. The B.A.A. added prize money to the race in 1986. Since then, runners have won more than $12 million.

2 Starting the Race

The Boston Marathon uses a special start system called the "wave start." Wheelchair athletes are first to start, followed 10 minutes later by the elite women runners. About 30 minutes after this, elite men start the race. At the same time, thousands of other runners, known as Wave 1, also begin running. The final group, Wave 2, starts a half hour later, completing the starting process.

3 The Race

During the race, runners are allowed to run as fast or as slow as they choose. A major part of marathon running is to keep a consistent, comfortable **pace**. Runners must remain on the course while running and must not **interfere** with other runners. Every participant in the marathon deserves the same respect.

4 Finishing the Race

Not every runner who starts the Boston Marathon makes it to the finish line. Each year, a number of runners drop out of the race because of injury, exhaustion, or other problems. In order to be an official finisher at the Boston Marathon, a runner must cross the finish line within six hours of starting. Some racers finish the course, but do not get official recognition because they took longer than the time limit to complete the race.

5 Timing

With so many people starting and finishing the race at the same time, it can be difficult to keep track of everyone. Each competitor in the Boston Marathon is assigned a number, which they wear on a bib. Officials keep track of the runners by their bib numbers. The numbers are recorded by wave. When runners cross the finish line, their number is recorded by timekeepers.

Champion Chip

Boston Marathon runners can participate in a program called Champion Chip, which allows their family and friends to keep track of their progress during the race. Runners taking part in the program are given a tiny electronic chip that attaches to their shoe. When the runner reaches certain points of the course, a text message is sent to family and friends, showing the runner's time and distance. The chip sends updates when the runner reaches 6.2 miles (10 km), 13.04 miles (21 km), 18.6 miles (30 km), and the finish line.

The Boston Marathon Route

T he Boston Marathon begins on Main Street in the town of Hopkinton, Massachusetts. The route winds through several communities that surround Boston, including Framingham, Wellesley, and Newton, before entering the city. The finish line is in front of the Boston Public Library on Boylston Street. The course contains several hills and valleys, similar to the original course in Greece.

Running the Race

This map shows the Boston Marathon route from Main Street in Hopkinton to central Boston.

Legend

- Country
- City
- Marathon Route
- Mile Marker

N
W — E
S

1 Mile
0   1.6 Kilometers

HOPKINTON

START

The Longest Yard

A National Football League (NFL) field is 100 yards (91 meters) long. The distance Boston Marathon runners race is the length of about 461 football fields laid end to end.

When the Boston Marathon was first held in 1897, the route was different from the one used today. The race began at a mill in Ashland, Massachusetts, and ended at the Irvington Oval, a running track in Boston. The finish line was later moved in front of the B.A.A. clubhouse. In 1924, the starting line was moved to Hopkinton. In 1927, the official marathon distance was changed to 26 miles, 385 yards (42.2 km).

FINISH

HEARTBREAK HILL

BOSTON

HALF WAY

Heartbreak Hill

The first 25 miles (40 km) of the marathon follow a series of winding roads that are mainly downhill. After the 25-mile (40-km) mark, runners reach the Newton Hills. Though the hills are not very steep, runners are exhausted at this point in the race. The final hill on the marathon course is known as Heartbreak Hill. It was given this nickname in 1936. That year, runner John A. Kelley caught up to race leader Ellison Brown. Kelley petted Brown's shoulder as he ran by. The gesture spurred Brown into action, and he raced past Kelley to the finish line. The loss is said to have "broke Kelley's heart."

Marathon Equipment

Running a marathon requires very little gear. The few pieces of equipment runners use are designed to help the athletes stay cool, dry, and comfortable.

A good pair of running shoes is the most important piece of equipment a runner can have. Running for 26 miles (42 km) can cause many problems for a runner's feet, ankles, knees, legs, hips, and back. Wearing a strong pair of shoes that offer **shock absorption** can help keep a runner's body safe from injury.

Running shoes offer strong ankle support to protect runners from the strains and sprains of rolled ankles. The soles of running shoes are soft but firm. They respond to changes in the ground while keeping the feet in a strong, safe position. A good pair of shoes will protect a runner's entire body from injuries caused by shock.

Spandex

GET CONNECTED

Visit **www.the runnersguide.com/ runninggear** to learn more about running equipment.

Running Shoes

Water Bottle

When people run for long distances, they sweat. Sweating can cause a runner to **dehydrate**. For this reason, runners wear as little clothing as possible, and the clothes they do wear are very lightweight. Spandex is a common material used in running clothes. It is strong and flexible, giving support to the runner's muscles while allowing the runner to move easily. Microfibers that keep runners cool while **wicking** sweat from the body are also commonly used in running clothes.

Many runners wear sweatbands around their head. Sweatbands **absorb** sweat so it does not run from the forehead into the runner's eyes. Sweat in the eyes can be uncomfortable and distracting for a runner.

Time Saver

A big part of running marathons is improving the time it takes to complete the course. Runners often wear a wristwatch or timer, and monitor their progress throughout the run. Experienced runners will know how quickly they should be completing certain distances. By timing themselves, they will know if they need to pick up the pace.

Qualifying to Run

About 25,000 people run the Boston Marathon every year. Some of the runners are considered elite athletes. Most of the other runners are people who enjoy the challenge and the excitement of finishing the world's best-known marathon. Every runner, regardless of age, division, or goals must qualify to run in the Boston Marathon.

Every person who wants to run in the Boston Marathon must first prove that they are fast enough to participate. Each year, cities around the world host their own marathons. Some of these marathons are recognized by the B.A.A as Boston Marathon qualifiers. Qualifying races can be found in many places, including Lowell, Massachusetts, and Tucson, Arizona, in the United States, as well as Toronto, Canada, and Berlin, Germany. A runner must complete one of these races within a certain time in order to qualify to race in Boston.

Runners must be at least 18 years old to run the Boston Marathon.

Tatiana Titova and Joseph Ngolepus won the Rock 'n' Roll San Diego marathon in 2004. The event is a Boston Marathon qualifying race and features live music along the race route.

Each year, people of all ages participate in the Boston Marathon. Each division, gender, and age group has its own qualifying time for the event. For men aged 18 to 34 to take part, they must complete a qualifying marathon in a time of 3:10:59 or faster. Women in the same age group are given 3:40:59 to qualify. Older age groups are given more time to qualify. The oldest age group is 80 years or older. Men in this group have 5:00:59 to qualify, while women are given 5:30:59. Disabled participants also have time limits.

Eight hours is the qualifying time limit for a runner with an artificial leg.

The Ribbon

The Boston Marathon finish line is marked by a line painted on the ground. Every runner who finishes the marathon crosses this line. A ribbon also hangs across this line. The first runner in each division to reach the finish line runs through the ribbon to become the Boston Marathon champion. Only the marathon winner in each division gets to break through the ribbon.

Where They Run

Boston has a population of about 574,000 people. About 5,000 people from Boston ran in the Boston Marathon in 2009.

Boston is one of the largest cities in the United States. The city is known for its rich history, which includes the **Boston Tea Party**. It also is home to some of the most successful and popular sports teams in history. These include the Boston Red Sox baseball team, the Celtics basketball team, the Bruins hockey team, and the New England Patriots football team.

Even with so many athletic teams hosting games and tournaments in Boston, the Boston Marathon is the city's biggest annual sporting event. The crowds that gather to watch the runners can be as large as 500,000.

People from all over the world journey to Boston to participate in the event. In 2009, of the 23,167 people who ran in the marathon, 80 percent came from outside of the Boston area. This means that about 18,500 tourists were in town to run in the marathon, each paying more than $100 to race.

Thousands more people travel to Boston to watch the marathon. Tourists pay for food, transportation, entertainment, and accommodation during their stay in the city. It is estimated that the 2009 marathon boosted the city's economy by $95 million.

While visiting Boston for the marathon, tourists must find accommodation. Boston is home to many luxurious hotels.

Boston Marathon Champions 2009–2010				
Year	Division	Winner	Time	Country
2010	Men's	Robert K. Cheruiyot	2:05:52	Kenya
2010	Women's	Teyba Erkesso	2:26:11	Ethiopia
2010	Men's Wheelchair	Ernst Van Dyk	1:26:53	South Africa
2010	Women's Wheelchair	Wakako Tsuchida	1:43:32	Japan
2009	Men's	Deriba Merga	2:08:42	Ethiopia
2009	Women's	Salina Kosgei	2:32:16	Kenya
2009	Men's Wheelchair	Ernst Van Dyk	1:33:29	South Africa
2009	Women's Wheelchair	Wakako Tsuchida	1:54:37	Japan

Mapping 10 Major Marathons Around the World

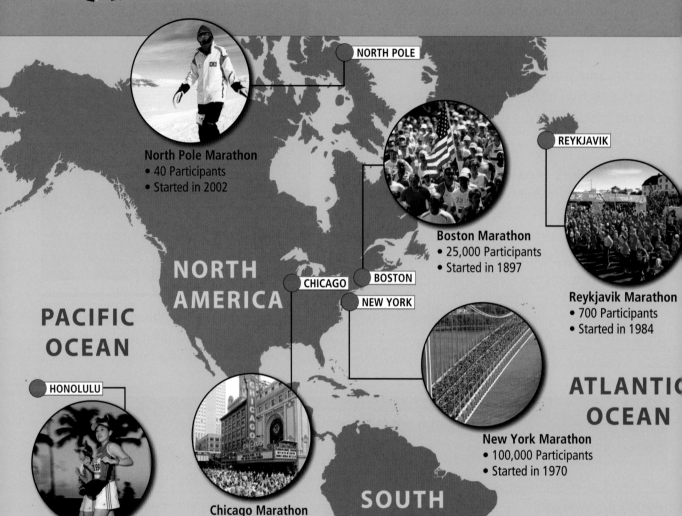

NORTH POLE

North Pole Marathon
- 40 Participants
- Started in 2002

Boston Marathon
- 25,000 Participants
- Started in 1897

REYKJAVIK

Reykjavik Marathon
- 700 Participants
- Started in 1984

NORTH AMERICA

PACIFIC OCEAN

CHICAGO

BOSTON

NEW YORK

ATLANTIC OCEAN

HONOLULU

New York Marathon
- 100,000 Participants
- Started in 1970

Honolulu Marathon
- 20,000 Participants
- Started in 1973

Chicago Marathon
- 40,000 Participants
- Started in 1977

SOUTH AMERICA

SOUTHERN OCEAN

The Boston Marathon is one of many well-known marathons around the world. Several cities in the United States and countries around the world hold marathons that draw runners from across the globe. This map shows where some of these marathons take place.

Legend

■ Continents

■ Oceans

● Marathon Location

621 Miles

0   1,000 Kilometers

N
W ● E
S

Edinburgh Marathon
- 13,000 Participants
- Started in 2003

ASIA

EDINBURGH

LONDON   BERLIN

EUROPE

Berlin Marathon
- 35,000 Participants
- Started in 1974

EVEREST

PACIFIC
OCEAN

AFRICA

INDIAN
OCEAN

AUSTRALIA

London Marathon
- 35,000 Participants
- Started in 1981

Everest Marathon
- 80 Participants
- Started in 1987

19

Women and the Boston Marathon

Each year, thousands of women enter the Boston Marathon. In 2009, of the 23,167 people who participated, 9,434 were women, with 9,298 finishing the race. The women's championship had a very exciting end, with three racers crossing the finish line very close together. Salina Kosgei of Kenya finished with a time of 2:32:16. She was only one second ahead of Dire Tune of Ethiopia. The third-place finisher, Kara Goucher of the United States, crossed the finish line nine seconds after Kosgei.

Until 1966, no women had ever participated in the Boston Marathon. In 1966, Roberta Gibb became the first woman to start and finish the race. However, she was not officially registered for the event because women were not allowed to compete. She had tried to register, but was declined by the B.A.A. It felt women could not handle the physical challenge. She wanted to prove women could run a marathon and decided to unofficially take part in the race.

Gibb hid in the bushes near the starting line, and when the race began, she joined the crowd of runners. The other racers soon offered their support, and women cheered Gibb on from the sidelines. She successfully finished the race in an unofficial time of 3:21:40, ahead of more than 60 percent of the other racers. Her story made newspaper headlines.

In 1983, Joan Benoit won the Boston Marathon for the second time. The next year, she became the first woman to win gold in an Olympic marathon.

GET CONNECTED

Read more about Roberta Gibb at **www.runningpast. com/gibb_story.htm.**

The next year, women were still not allowed to register for the event. Gibb once again ran unofficially. That same year, Kathrine Switzer became the first woman to register for the Boston Marathon. On her registration form, she entered her name as K. Switzer and did not clarify her gender.

Switzer was given an official number and bib, without ever being identified as a woman. As she reached the 4-mile (6.4-km) mark in the race, officials realized that there was a woman registered in the marathon. They tried to stop her from running. At one point, an official tried to physically remove Switzer from the race. Switzer had been running with her boyfriend, and he fought off the official. Switzer finished the marathon with an unofficial time of about 4:20:00. Gibb finished about one hour before Switzer.

Uta Pippig was the first woman to officially win the marathon three times in a row.

Making it Official

In 1972, women were finally allowed to register for the Boston Marathon. Nina Kuscsik of New York became the first official women's winner of the event, finishing with a time of 3:10:26. Pioneers, such as Roberta Gibb, Kathrine Switzer, and Sara Mae Berman, challenged the rules of the Boston Marathon, making it a competition for the best runners in the world, no matter their gender.

Historical Highlights

The first B.A.A. half marathon was run in 2001. A half marathon is 13.1 miles (21 km) long.

When the Boston Marathon was first run in 1897, it was only the second marathon in the world, and the first annual marathon in the United States. Today, cities in every state in the nation host annual marathons. While Boston is still the most recognized race, other marathons have grown to even larger sizes. Chicago hosts about 45,000 runners each year for the Chicago Marathon. The New York Marathon, which began in 1970, attracted more than 100,000 runners in 2009.

Although it has been run annually since 1897, the Boston Marathon has not always had the same name. Originally, it was named the American Marathon and was the final event of an Olympic-style festival called the B.A.A. Games.

The 1980 Boston Marathon is known for the Rosie Ruiz scandal. Ruiz finished the marathon before any other women and was declared the champion. However, race officials wondered why she was barely sweating after hours of running. They checked photographs of the race and could not find any evidence that she had run the entire course. Ruiz jumped into the race only half a mile (0.8 km) before the finish. She was stripped of her championship title and banned from the Boston Marathon. Officials also found out that Ruiz had cheated in the New York Marathon to qualify for the Boston event.

The Boston Marathon celebrated its 100th anniversary in 1996. A record 35,868 runners finished the race.

Prize money was first introduced to the Boston Marathon 89 years after it began. The women's champion in 1986, Ingrid Kristiansen of Norway, won $35,000 and a new car. The men's champion, Australian Robert de Castella, won a new car and $60,000. In 2009, both the male and female Boston Marathon winners were awarded $150,000.

Boston Marathon Records				
Event	Time	Runner	Country	Year
Men's Open	2:05:52	Robert K. Cheruiyot	Kenya	2010
Women's Open	2:20:43	Margaret Okayo	Kenya	2002
Men's Wheelchair	1:18:27	Ernst Van Dyk	South Africa	2004
Women's Wheelchair	1:34:22	Jean Driscoll	United States	1994

LEGENDS and Current Stars

Catherine Ndereba

Robert K. Cheruiyot

Robert K. Cheruiyot

Robert K. Cheruiyot has won the Boston Marathon five times, more than any other Kenyan. Cheruiyot first won the Boston Marathon in 2003, when he finished in 2:10:11. It was the 12th time in 13 years that a Kenyan man had won the marathon. In 2006, Cheruiyot won his second Boston Marathon, setting a course record of 2:07:14. He finished the race one second faster than the old record, held by fellow Kenyan and three-time Boston Marathon champion, Cosmas Ndeti. The following year, Cheruiyot won again. This time, he ran through wind, rain, and cold to become the eighth man to win more than two Boston Marathons. In 2008, Cheruiyot made history once more, becoming the youngest man to win the Boston Marathon four times. He was 29 years old. Cheruiyot finished in 2:07:46, 78 seconds ahead of the second-place finisher. In 2010, Cheruiyot won the marathon a fifth time.

Catherine Ndereba

Catherine Ndereba was born to run. As a girl growing up in Kenya, she felt the urge to run every day. "Something was in my blood," she said, "I could not part with it." Ndereba would run before and after school. Ndereba's dedication and love for running has shown in her ability to excel at the sport. In 2000, she won her first Boston Marathon, finishing in 2:26:11. In 2001, Ndereba finished even faster, with a time of 2:23:53. Later that year, Ndereba ran an even faster time. At the Chicago Marathon in October, Ndereba became only the second woman to run a marathon in less than 2:20:00. She finished the Chicago Marathon in a world record time of 2:18:47. Ndereba returned to Boston to win the 2004 marathon, with a time of 2:24:27. It was her third championship. The following year, she once again made history, becoming the first woman to win the Boston Marathon four times. She finished in 2:25:13.

Dick and Rick Hoyt

Dick and Rick Hoyt, known as Team Hoyt, are an example of dedication and teamwork. They have inspired millions of people around the world to overcome **adversity** and meet challenges by participating in marathons and **triathlons** across the country. In 1962, Dick and Judy Hoyt had a son named Rick. Rick was born a **quadriplegic** with **cerebral palsy**. He was unable to talk. With the help of a special computer, Rick spoke his first words at the age of 10. He surprised his parents by saying, "Go Bruins," when cheering for Boston's NHL team. In 1977, Rick asked his dad to help him run 5 miles (8 km) to raise money for a lacrosse player who had become **paralyzed**. Dick ran while pushing Rick in his wheelchair. This was the beginning of Team Hoyt. The 2009 Boston Marathon was the 1,000th race for Team Hoyt.

Ernst Van Dyk

South Africa's Ernst Van Dyk won his first men's wheelchair championship in 2001, in a time of 1:25:12. Van Dyk also won six Boston Marathons, from 2001 to 2006. In 2007, he lost his title as Boston Marathon champion, but he trained hard and regained his Boston title in 2008. In 2009, Van Dyk won his eighth Boston Marathon, finishing in 1:33:29. He won for the ninth time in 2010, with a time of 1:26:53. Van Dyk's 2004 time of 1:18:27 still stands as the course record for the wheelchair division.

Ernst Van Dyk

Dick and Rick Hoyt

Famous Firsts

John Caffery won the Boston Marathon in 1900 and 1901. Since then, several runners have won the marathon consecutively. Aurele Vandendriessche of Belgium won the Boston Marathon in 1963 and 1964.

With thousands of people competing in the Boston Marathon each year, history can be made at any moment.

In 1901, John Vrazanis of Greece became the first person from outside North America to enter the race. Vrazanis dropped out of the race due to severe blisters. That year, John Caffery became the first runner to win the Boston Marathon more than once. He finished the marathon in 2:29:23, shaving 10 minutes off his championship time from the previous year.

Caffery was also the first runner to finish the Boston Marathon in less than 2:30:00. The last time a men's open champion took longer than 2:30:00 to run the marathon was in 1952, when Doroteo Flores of Guatemala finished in 2:31:53.

The first time a Kenyan runner won the Boston Marathon was in 1988. Since then, Kenyans have dominated the men's open division, winning 16 more championships in Boston.

The Boston Marathon has been an international affair since the very beginning. The first foreign champion was Ronald MacDonald, a student from Nova Scotia, Canada. He won in 1898. Since then, 19 countries have been represented by a champion.

The United States has the most champions in total, but a representative from this nation has not won a championship since 1985. This is when Michigan's Lisa Larsen-Weidenbach finished with a time of 2:34:06. The last men's champion from the United States was Boston's Greg Meyer, who finished the 1983 marathon in 2:09:00.

In 1999, Australia's Louise Sauvage narrowly edged out Jean Driscoll of the United States to win the women's wheelchair division of the Boston Marathon. One year earlier, both women received the exact same finish time.

Finishing First

On Patriots' Day, April 19, 1897, 15 runners took part in the first-ever Boston Marathon. Only 10 runners finished the race. John J. McDermott was crowned champion, finishing with a time of 2:55:10. He won by nearly seven minutes over the next competitor, Dick Grant. McDermott, who traveled from New York to run, was the first winner of the Boston Marathon. Through the years, with more participants, better techniques, and better equipment, champions have become faster. Today, champions finish the race in much less time. In order to win the Boston Marathon, a runner should aim for a finishing time of less than 2:10:00.

The Rise of the Marathon

1918

Due to World War I, the Boston Marathon is not held. Instead, a **relay** marathon between teams of 10 soldiers is held. Camp Devens, from Massachusetts, is the winning team.

1896

After witnessing the first marathon at the Olympics, John Graham decides to bring a marathon to Boston.

1924

The length of the course is changed to 26 miles, 385 yards (42.2 km), and the start line is moved from Ashland to Hopkinton.

1887

The Boston Athletic Association (B.A.A.) is formed to promote healthy, active lifestyles in Boston.

1897

The first Boston Marathon is held on Patriots' Day, April 19, and won by John J. McDermott.

1966

Roberta Gibb sneaks into the race to become the first woman to run the Boston Marathon.

1988

Ibrahim Hussein is the first African champion.

2005

The first Boston Marathon is held in Tallil, Iraq. Forty-one American soldiers take part.

970

or the first time, runners must qualify or the Boston Marathon.

972

Vomen are officially allowed o compete. Nina Kuscsik becomes he first official women's champion.

986

rize money is awarded for the irst time.

1996

The 100th anniversary run sees 35,868 people finish the race. This is the largest field in history.

2006

The wave start is introduced.

QUICK FACTS

- The Boston Marathon is the only annual marathon in the world that requires qualification.

- Every year, the Boston Marathon is run on the third Monday of April, Patriots' Day.

- The Boston Marathon is the second-most watched single-day sporting event in the United States, behind the Super Bowl.

Test Your Knowledge

7 Who was the first person from outside the United States to win the Boston Marathon?

8 Who was the last American women's open champion at the Boston Marathon?

1 What is the name of the town where Pheidippides started his well-known run?

2 What organization hosts the Boston Marathon each year?

3 What is the name of the start system used at the Boston Marathon?

4 Where does the Boston Marathon begin?

5 Who was the first woman to run the Boston Marathon?

6 Who was the first woman to be given an official number in the Boston Marathon?

9 What is the Boston Marathon men's open record, and who holds it?

10 Who was the first person to win the Boston Marathon?

Further Research

Many books and websites provide information on the Boston Marathon. To learn more about the race, borrow books from the library, or surf the Internet.

Books to Read

Most libraries have computers that connect to a database for researching information. If you input a key word, you will be provided with a list of books in the library that contain information on that topic. Non-fiction books are arranged numerically, using their call number. Fiction books are organized alphabetically by the author's last name.

Online Sites

The Boston Athletic Association website contains a great deal about the history of the event and about this year's race. Visit www.bostonmarathon.org

Learn how to get involved in running events at http://news.youthrunner.com

Find out more about Boston at www.cityofboston.gov

Glossary

absorb: to sop up

adversity: difficulty

annual: held every year

Boston Tea Party: an event in 1773 in which residents of Boston tossed tea off three British ships in protest of a tax on tea

cerebral palsy: a condition caused by brain damage that affects the muscles

dehydrate: to lose water from the body

elite: the best runners

entrepreneurs: people who organize and operate businesses

exhaustion: being extremely tired or exhausted

interfere: to prevent another runner from running

mahogany: a type of red tropical wood used for building quality goods

mobility impaired: people who have conditions that make running difficult

modern: present times, rather than ancient times

pace: a steady speed of running

paralyzed: unable to use certain areas of the body

quadriplegic: a person who cannot use their arms or legs

relay: a race where one person runs a certain distance before being replaced by a teammate

shock absorption: cushioning

sterling: the best quality silver

triathlons: races that include swimming, cycling, and running

visually impaired: people with conditions that make them blind or partially blind

wicking: pulling sweat away from the body

Index